Toad and I

LOUISE YATES

Jonathan Cape
London

For Pat White

TOAD AND I

A JONATHAN CAPE BOOK 978 1 780 08105 2

Published in Great Britain by Jonathan Cape,

an imprint of Random House Children's Publishers UK

A Penguin Random House Company

This edition published 2016

1 3 5 7 9 10 8 6 4 2

RANDOM HOUSE CHILDREN'S PUBLISHERS UK

61–63 Uxbridge Road, London W5 5SA

www.**randomhousechildrens**.co.uk

www.**randomhouse**.co.uk

Addresses for companies within The Random House Group Limited can be found at:

www.randomhouse.co.uk/offices.htm

THE RANDOM HOUSE GROUP Limited Reg. No. 954009

A CIP catalogue record for this book is available from the British Library.

Printed in China

Penguin Random House is committed to a sustainable future for our business,
our readers and our planet. This book is made from Forest Stewardship Council® certified paper.

One day, Kitty was playing with her new
bouncy ball when she bounced it a bit too hard
and it flew over the fence and disappeared.

So she went to look for it.

"HELLO,"
said a voice.

"Hello," said Kitty.
"Who's there?"

It was a toad.

Kitty kissed him to
see if he would
turn into a
prince . . .

. . . but he didn't.

"What are you
doing in a tree?"
she asked.
"Lots!" he said.
"Come in and see."

"Behold! My treehouse!"
boomed Toad. "Follow me!"

POOL

KITCHEN

LABORATORY

OBSERVATORY

LOUNGE

ICE-CREAM PARLOUR

IN

OUT

LOO

Toad was showing Kitty around
when a squirrel burst in.

"Toad, fetch the doctor quick!"
said Squirrel.
"Owl's been hit on the head!"
"To the Dressing-Up Chamber!" cried Toad.

He and Kitty quickly ran to another room.

When they'd finished dressing up,
they ran to find Owl.

Owl was outside. "Owl!" said Toad.
"What hit you?"

"A meteorite," said Owl. "It knocked me off
my branch."
"To the Observatory!" cried Toad.

Toad was looking for more meteorites

when a shrew ran in.

"Toad!" said Shrew. "Come quickly! My house has been squashed by a MONSTER!"

"Everyone to the Armoury!" cried Toad. "We must trap the monster with sticky tape."

Outside, the search party spread out. "Toad, come quickly!" called Rabbit, and pointed to a prickly creature curled up in the leaves.

"Hedgehog!" said Toad. "Are you all right? Were you hit by a meteorite? Were you mashed by a monster?"

"I'm not sure," he said. "Whatever it was bashed me on my behind – I curled up as quick as I could."

"Hush!" said Rabbit. "I can hear . . .

. . . hissing!"

Hisssssssssssssssssssss...

"It's a snake!" shouted Toad.
"Don't worry, I know what to do."

Toad made a musical instrument from twigs and
sticky tape. "Stand back," he said.
"I'm going to charm it."

They all stood well back.

Hissssssssssssssssssss...

"I don't think it's working, Toad," said Kitty.

"It's not a snake!" screamed Birdy suddenly. "It's a cat!"

Everyone panicked.

Everyone except Kitty.
"Well, I'm not afraid of cats, snakes,
meteorites or monsters," she said,
and went to find out what it was once
and for all. "Aha!" she cried. "It's . . ."

"A meteorite?" hooted Owl.

"A monster?" shivered Shrew.

"A cat!" screamed Birdy.

"It's a snake," said Toad.

"No," said Kitty. "It's my . . .

. . . BALL!"

It was the ball that had
bounced over
the fence,

bowled Owl off her branch,

squashed
Shrew's house,

hit Hedgehog and hissed like a snake
when his prickles punctured it!

Hisssssss...

"I'm sorry," said Kitty, but no one seemed to mind.
It was only a ball, after all!

In the workshop, Kitty and Toad mended the ball

and built Shrew a new house. Then . . .

. . . they played!

But before long it was time for Kitty
to go home for her tea.

"Would you like some worms?"
asked Toad.

"No, thanks," she said.

"When will you be back?" he asked.

"Soon," she said.

"Good," said Toad, and then he kissed her.

"I wasn't trying to turn you into a princess,"
he said. "Just saying goodbye."

"Goodbye, Toad," she called as she crawled
back through the hole in the fence.

"Wait!" he called after her.
"You forgot your ball!"
And then he bounced it . . .

. . . a bit too hard.